collected by
Zora Neale Hurston

What's The Hurry, Fox?
AND OTHER ANIMAL STORIES

illustrated by **Bryan Collier**
adapted by **Joyce Carol Thomas**

HARPERCOLLINSPUBLISHERS

For my nine-year-old cousin,
Ashlee Cole, with love
—J.C.T.

With love and celebration, I dedicate this book
to all of the families and friends from my neighborhood.
It is through these tales that you finally have
the ear of the world.
—B.C.

*The Zora Neale Hurston Trust gratefully thanks Joyce Carol Thomas and Bryan Collier
for their superb work. The Trust is also very thankful for the vision and guidance of Susan Katz,
Kate Jackson, and our wonderful editor, Phoebe Yeh. Lastly, as always, our continued appreciation of
Cathy Hemming and Jane Friedman, who daily work tirelessly on behalf of Zora.*

Sources as they appeared in *Every Tongue Got to Confess: Negro Folk-tales from the Gulf States:*
"Why the Buzzard Has No Home": Armetta Jones, age 42, domestic, Georgia born;
"What's the Hurry, Fox?," "Why Porpoise's Tail Is on Crosswise," "Why Flies Get the First Taste": M. C. Ford;
"Why Donkey Has Long Ears": Nathaniel Burney, age 9, schoolboy, Florida born;
"Why the Dog Hates the Cat": Mack C. Ford, age 55, gardener, Florida;
"Why the Waves Have Whitecaps": Lily May Beale;
"Why Frog Got Eyes and Mole Got Tail": M. C. Yard.

What's the Hurry, Fox? And Other Animal Stories
Text copyright © 2004 by Zora Neale Hurston Trust
Adapter's copyright © 2004 by Joyce Carol Thomas
Illustrations copyright © 2004 by Bryan Collier
Manufactured in China by South China Printing Company Ltd. All rights reserved.
www.harperchildrens.com

Library of Congress Cataloging-in-Publication Data
Thomas, Joyce Carol.
  What's the hurry, Fox? : and other animal stories / collected by Zora Neale Hurston ; adapted by Joyce Carol Thomas ; illustrated by Bryan
Collier. — 1st ed.
    p.   cm.
  Summary: Presents a volume of pourquoi tales collected by Zora Neale Hurston from her field research in the Gulf states in the 1930s.
  ISBN 0-06-000643-9 — ISBN 0-06-000644-7 (lib. bdg.)
  1. Children's stories, American. 2. Tales—United States. 3. African Americans—Folklore. [1. Folklore—United States. 2. African
Americans—Folklore. 3. Short stories.] I. Hurston, Zora Neale. II. Collier, Bryan, ill. III. Title.
PZ8.1.T3765Wh 2004
398.2'0973'0452—dc21
                                                                                                                          2003007147

Typography by Matt Adamec
1 2 3 4 5 6 7 8 9 10
❖
First Edition

Zora Neale Hurston is a gift! Through her folksy collection of rich words falling like diamonds from the mouths of poor people, she joyfully shares the stories of a colorful America.

As I recite these adapted pourquoi tales to children, they flap their wings like Buzzard and giggle in all the funny-bone places. They read along with Rooster and Fox. They jump like Frog, sparkle like Water, and dance like Wind.

Wise, witty, and wonderful! Zora Neale Hurston has left us a library of everyday humor from everyday people, who tell us why Donkey's ears are long and why Dog hates Cat.

Zora Neale Hurston has willed us a legacy of laughter.

In my adaptation I pass along *What's the Hurry, Fox?*, custom-made for a child's eye and ear and shaped just so for a child's gentle bursts of laughter.

—Joyce Carol Thomas

I was raised in rural southern Maryland (Pocomoke City), and my neighborhood was made up of mostly older retirees. These older folks often told funny yet familiar stories. And from being in their presence, I know that they embodied all of the wit and charm that Zora Neale Hurston found in these tales.

—Bryan Collier

Why the Buzzard Has No Home

Every time it rains, Buzzard says, "Just as soon as it stops all this raining, I'm sure gonna build me a house."

But just as soon as the weather fairs off, Buzzard says, "Who wants any old house? The air's too sweet to be sittin' inside anyhow. I wouldn't be bothered."

But just as soon as it starts raining again, he starts moaning, "If the weather ever fairs off, I'm sure gonna build me a house."

What's the Hurry, Fox?

A bunch of Hens and a Rooster out by the chicken shack weren't roosting very high. Fox would go there every morning and catch one of Rooster's Hens.

Rooster said, "I'm gonna change my roosting place."

So the very next morning Fox found Rooster roosting way up in the tree, looking down on him. "Good morning, Brer Rooster," said Fox. "Have I got good news for you! Come on down so I can tell you."

"I don't wanna come on down right now."

"Why not?" asked Brer Fox.

"It's too early in the day, Brer Fox. I can listen right here. So what's the news you're holding for me?"

Fox said, "The law's gone and changed. Now Fox eats no more Roosters. And Hounds run no more Foxes. Ain't that *good* news?"

While they were talking, they heard the Hounds holler, "Ow-ooo …"

Fox said, "Hush, Brer Rooster, what's that noise?"

Rooster said, "That ain't nothing but the Hounds."

Fox said, "Well, believe I'll hurry along now."

Brer Rooster said, "What's the hurry, Brer Fox? Didn't you just tell me the new law says Hounds run no more Foxes?"

Brer Fox said as he took off running, "Yeah, but them Hounds liable to run all over that law and break it clean in two."

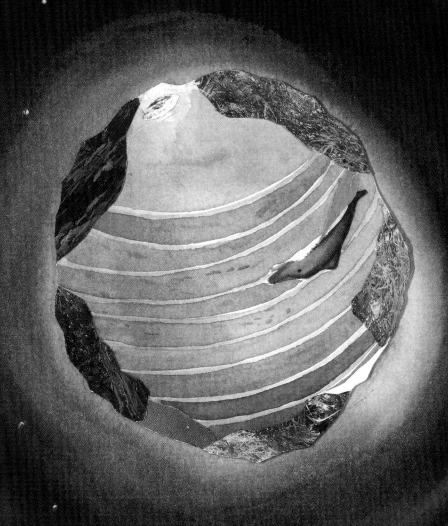

Why Porpoise's Tail Is on Crosswise

I want to tell you about Porpoise. God had made the world and everything. He'd already set the moon and the stars in the sky. He finished with the fishes of the sea and the fowls of the air.

He made the Sun and hung the Sun up in the sky. Then he made a nice gold track for the Sun to run on.

Then He said, "Now, Sun, I got everything made but Time. That's up to you. I want you to start out and go 'round the world on this gold track just as fast as you can. And the Time it takes you to go, I'm gonna call that Time day. And the Time it takes you to come back, I'm gonna call that Time night."

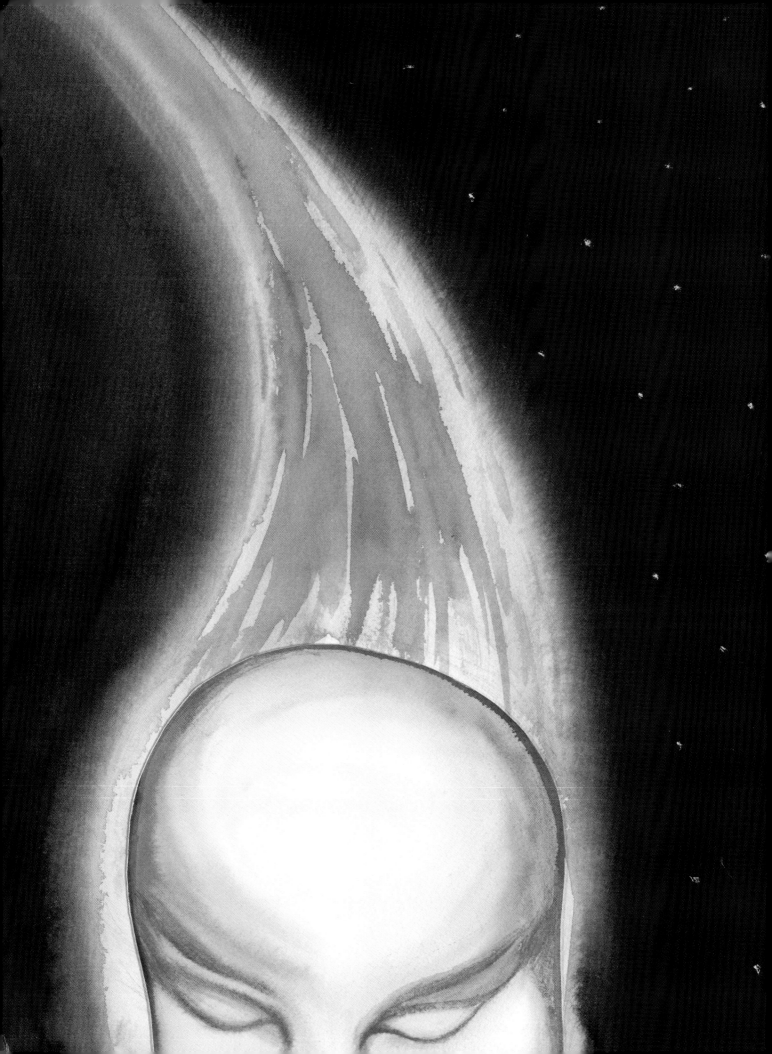

The Sun nodded his head and went zooming on 'cross the elements.

Now Porpoise was hanging around there and heard what God told the Sun. So Porpoise decided he'd take that same trip and race the Sun 'round the world.

He looked up and saw the Sun kiting along, so he lit out too, flying so fast he caught up with the Sun. Him and that Sun neck and neck! Then Porpoise passed the Sun!

Porpoise beat the Sun around the world by one hour and three minutes.

God leaned back and said, "Aw no, this ain't gonna do! I didn't mean for nothing to be faster than the Sun!"

So God ran after Porpoise for three days before He caught Porpoise, took his tail off, and put it on crossways. Yet and still, Porpoise might be slow on land but when it comes to being in the water, he's the fastest thing running.

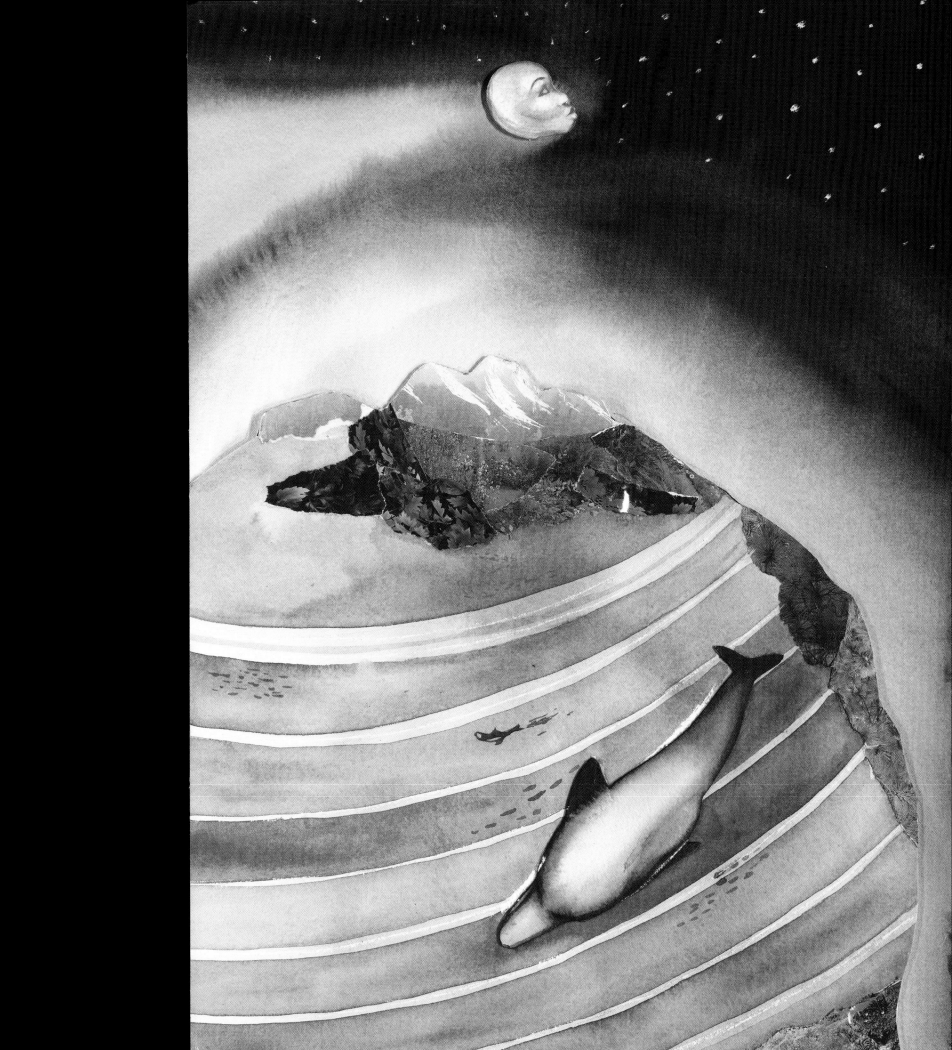

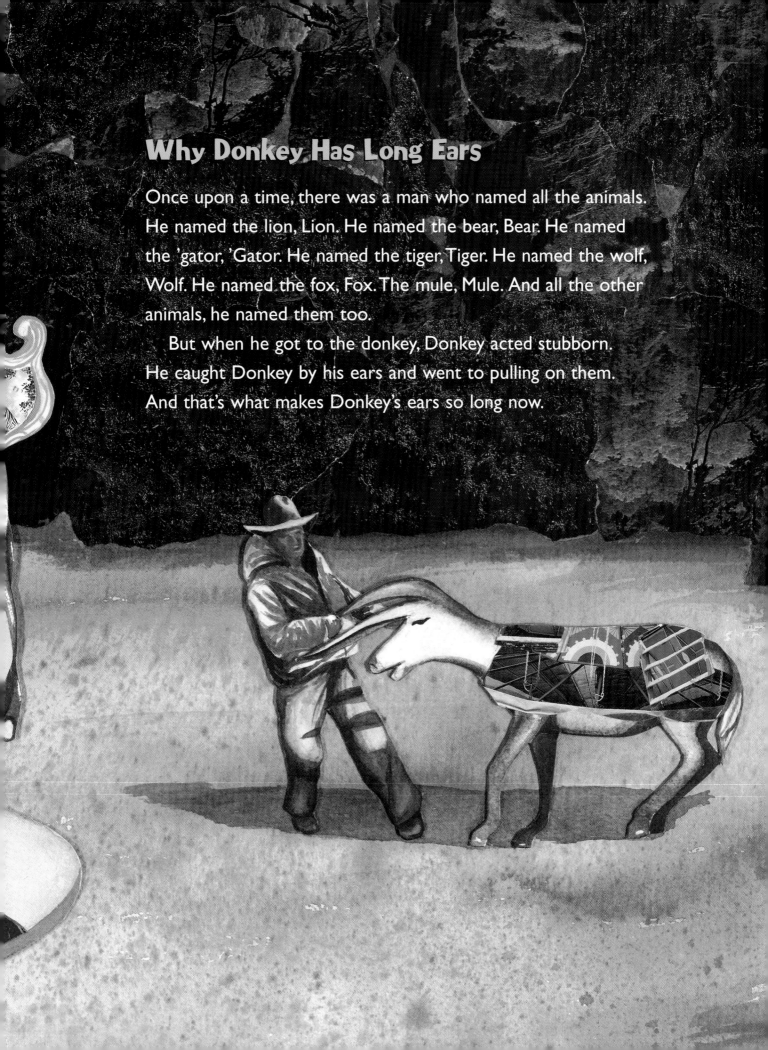

Why Donkey Has Long Ears

Once upon a time, there was a man who named all the animals.
He named the lion, Lion. He named the bear, Bear. He named
the 'gator, 'Gator. He named the tiger, Tiger. He named the wolf,
Wolf. He named the fox, Fox. The mule, Mule. And all the other
animals, he named them too.

But when he got to the donkey, Donkey acted stubborn.
He caught Donkey by his ears and went to pulling on them.
And that's what makes Donkey's ears so long now.

Why the Dog Hates the Cat

Cat and Dog were good friends one time. Both of them loved ham. So they put in together and went downtown and bought them a ham. Dog toted it first. He said, "Our ham, our ham, ours, ours, ours."

Come time for Cat to tote it awhile, she says, "My ham, my ham, my ham."

Dog toted it again. He says, "Ours, ours, ours."

Cat took it again. She says, "My ham, my ham."

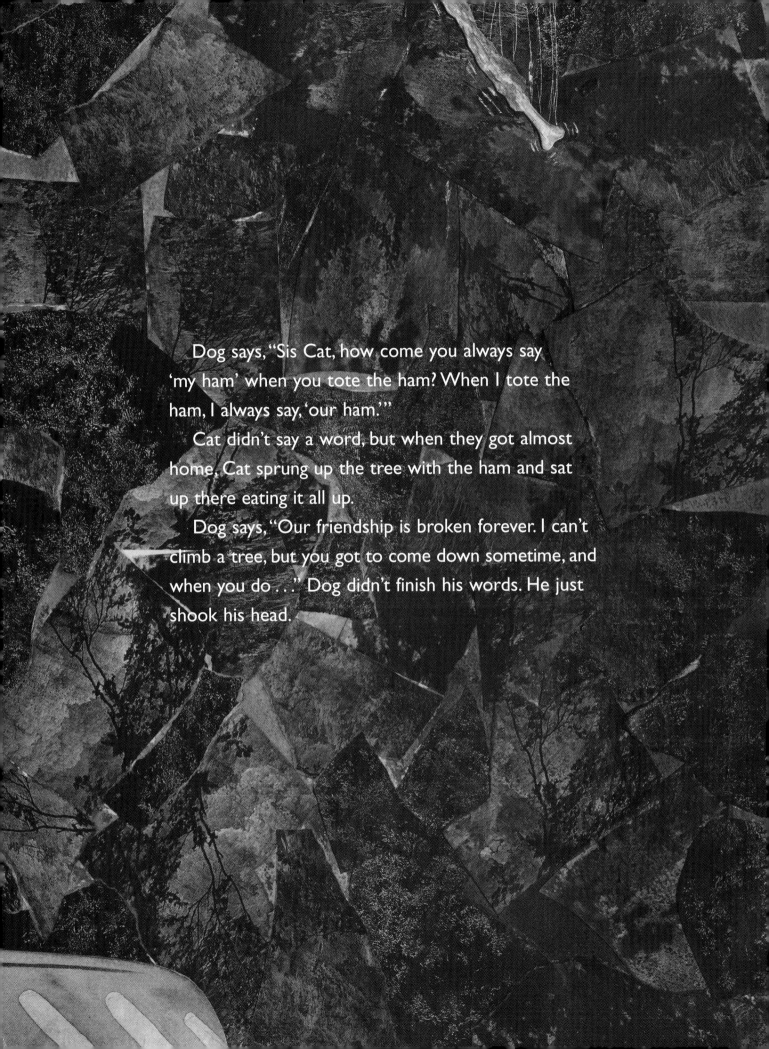

Dog says, "Sis Cat, how come you always say 'my ham' when you tote the ham? When I tote the ham, I always say, 'our ham.'"

Cat didn't say a word, but when they got almost home, Cat sprung up the tree with the ham and sat up there eating it all up.

Dog says, "Our friendship is broken forever. I can't climb a tree, but you got to come down sometime, and when you do . . ." Dog didn't finish his words. He just shook his head.

Why the Waves Have Whitecaps

Now Wind and Water were both women. They both had children.
   Wind told Water, "My children, they're better than yours. Some fly
in the air. Some walk on the ground. And some swim in the water.
Yours can't do nothing but swim."

Water got mad at Wind for talking like that just because she was Wind, and therefore the mother of all the birds.

So the very next time a lot of birds came down from the sky to drink, Water caught every last one of Wind's children and drowned them.

Wind knew she had left her children down by the water, so she kept passing over, calling her children. Every time she called them, the waves stirred up and Wind's children showed their white feathers to let their mother know where they were, but Water wouldn't let them go.

Even today, every time you see the waves bucking and showing their whitecaps in the storm, it's Water and Wind fighting about the children.

Why Frog Got Eyes and Mole Got Tail

Frog used to have a long big tail and no eyes. Mole was the opposite. Mole had eyes and no tail.

So one day Mole came up out of the ground with his eyes full of dirt. He just kept wiping his eyes and getting the sand out so he could see.

Soon as Mole could see everything, he looked around and saw Frog sitting up with his big tail and no eyes.

So Mole said, "Say, Brer Frog, what you want with that big old tail anyway? Ain't no good to you."

Frog said, "Say, Brer Mole, what you want with them eyes and live in the dark all the time? Besides, you roots your way and gets them eyes full of dirt."

Mole said, "Let's swap, Brer Frog."

So they did. Now Frog got eyes and no tail and Mole got tail and no eyes.

Why Flies Get the First Taste

The Flies were so small that everything trod on them and kept them back from the table. So the Flies had a conference—they wanted to know what to do.

So the Flies said, "We'll go up to Heaven and tell God about it."

So they flew, one right behind the other, one right after the other, until they reached Heaven, where they had a conference with God.

The Flies said, "Lord, we ain't got no weapons to fight with and no way to protect ourselves, and we can't get nothing to eat."

So God said, "Go on home to Earth, and when you get back I'll fix it so you'll get the first taste of everything."

So the Flies flew home, and now they never fail.
The Flies swarm over everybody's food before they
can even take the first bite.

Why the Buzzard Has No Home

Every time it rained, Buzzard said, "Soon as it stops raining, I'm sure enough gonna build me a house."

But as soon as the weather faired off, Buzzard said, "Who wants any old house? The air is too sweet to be sittin' inside anyhow. I wouldn't be bothered."

Zora Neale Hurston 1891–1960